When a TV ad tells you THESE SHOES WILL NEVER WEAR OUT, do not believe them.

When you have Destructo-feet, anything is possible.

ROSCOE RILEY

Rules

#6

Never Walk in Shoes that Talk

Katherine Applegate

illustrated by Brian Biggs

HarperCollins*Publishers*

For Anne H.,
Roscoe's Fairy Godmother

Roscoe Riley Rules #6:
Never Walk in Shoes that Talk
Text copyright © 2009 by Katherine Applegate
Illustrations copyright © 2009 by Brian Biggs

Library of Congress Cataloging-in-Publication Data
Applegate, Katherine.
  Never walk in shoes that talk / Katherine Applegate ; illustrated
by Brian Biggs. — 1st ed.
    p. cm. — (Roscoe Riley rules ; #6)
  Summary: Having gotten a pair of hard-to-find Walkie Talkie
shoes, Roscoe is suddenly popular and wants his best friend, Gus,
to join the fun, but before Gus's parents will buy him new shoes,
he must wear out his long-lasting sneakers.
  ISBN 978-0-06-114891-0 (pbk.)
  ISBN 978-0-06-114892-7 (trade bdg.)
  [1. Shoes—Fiction. 2. Popularity—Fiction. 3. Schools—Fiction.
4. Humorous stories.] I. Biggs, Brian, ill. II. Title.
PZ7.A6483New 2009   2008024128
[Fic]—dc22   CIP
                                                          AC

    09 10 11 12 13   LP/RRDB   10 9 8 7 6 5 4 3 2 1
                              ❖
                       First Edition

Contents

1

Welcome to Time-Out

You know, being stuck in time-out isn't so bad.

If you bring your imagination along for company.

Like right now.

I may *look* like I'm just sitting in my time-out corner.

But I'm pretending I'm playing baseball.

I just hit sixteen home runs in a row!

I am a baseball superstar.

I have a gazillion fans. I'm a very cool guy.

Inside my brain, anyway.

In real life, I'm a pretty ordinary guy, to tell the truth.

Although last week, I was one of the coolest kids in class for a while.

Actually, being cool is why I'm here in time-out.

Well, that's not exactly the reason.

I guess maybe the part where I destroyed my friend Gus's sneakers might have something to do with it.

I was just trying to help Gus be cool too.

You've smushed up shoes for a good reason before, haven't you?

No?

Not even to help out your best buddy?

I guess maybe this *does* sound a little strange.

Maybe I should back up a bit.

To when this all started.

The part before I was cool for two whole days.

Something You Should Know
Before We Get Started

When a TV ad tells you THESE SHOES WILL NEVER WEAR OUT, do not believe them.

When you have Destructo-feet, anything is possible.

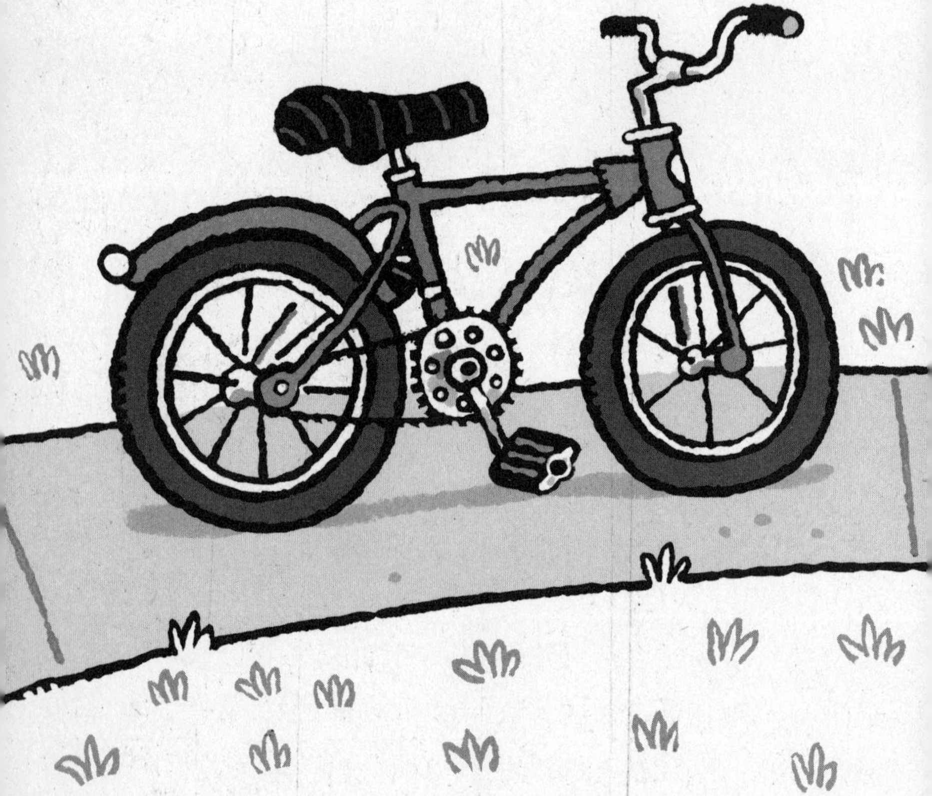

Something Else
You Should Know
Before We Get Started

If you want to stop your bike, use your brakes.

Do not drag your toes on the ground to make it stop.

That is why brakes were invented.

That is all I have to say on the subject.

4

Uncool Shoes

Everything started one morning when I was putting my backpack in my cubby at school.

I heard Gus shout my name.

"Roscoe! You gotta see this! Hassan and Coco have talking shoes!"

Gus grabbed my arm and pulled. "Come on! This is major!"

Gus says lots of crazy things.

Once he told me he was pretty sure his guinea pig could count to ten in Spanish.

So when he told me two kids in our class had talking shoes, I wasn't all that surprised.

"They're called Walkie-Talkies," Gus said. "I saw them on TV. You will not believe the amazingness of these shoes!"

We ran into class.

And there before me was a whole new world of shoe possibilities.

Kids surrounded Hassan and Coco, who were each wearing a kind of sneaker I'd never seen before.

The shoes were made of shiny plastic. Like the boots my sister wears when it rains.

On one shoe was a big *W*.

On the other shoe was a big *T*.

There was a black push button near the toe of each shoe.

Coco's sneakers were pink. With glitter shoelaces.

Hassan's sneakers were blue with

lightning stripes.

Coco and Hassan were sitting in chairs on opposite sides of the room.

Coco had her left leg crossed over her knee.

She was whispering something into her shoe.

Which I have to admit looked pretty weird.

Hassan had his right leg crossed over his knee.

And here's the can-you-believe-it thing: Coco's voice was coming out of Hassan's shoe!

"See?" Gus whispered. "Walkie-Talkies! You talk into that little circle on the left shoe. It's sort of like talking into a cell phone. And if you have a friend with a pair of Walkie-Talkies on, they can hear you out of a little bitty speaker in their right toe!"

I did not even know what to say.

It was a science miracle.

Better even than Silly Putty.

Coco whispered something to her foot.

Hassan's shoe said, "I just *love* my Walkie-Talkies!"

Hassan's shoe.

Coco's voice.

Hassan grinned. "My dad got mine in Los Angeles on a business trip. Last time he just brought me a pack of peanuts and a cocktail napkin."

"Wow," I said.

"Yeah," Hassan agreed. "The only bad thing is that they are kind of uncomfortable. I have three blisters already."

"I have four," Coco said.

We sat there, oohing and aahing.

I knew what we were all thinking.

We were wondering what we could say to our parents that might make *them* say, "Hmm, this kid is so sweet I think I will run to the nearest store and buy him some Walkie-Talkies before they are all sold out."

I tried hard to think of something sweet to tell my dad.

He is getting balder every day.

Maybe I could tell him I'd noticed some fresh hair sprouts.

"My mom bought the last pair at Shoe Palace," Coco said. "They said they might get some more next week."

Ms. Diz, our teacher, came over to see what all the fuss was about.

"Why are you talking to your shoes?"

she asked in a polite way.

"This is the latest in fashion footwear, Ms. Diz!" said Coco.

"I can talk to Coco from anywhere in the room," Hassan said.

Ms. Diz frowned.

"Hmm. I'm not sure teachers are going to be too thrilled about this idea," she

said. "I liked the last shoe fad better. The ones that lit up. At least they were quiet!"

"What's a fad?" I asked.

"It's something that's very popular," Emma answered.

Emma knows all kinds of interesting words.

"Fads don't usually last very long," Ms. Diz added.

"I saw an ad for Walkie-Talkies on TV yesterday and asked my mom if I could get some," Gus said. "She said no. And then Babette spit up on Mom's bathrobe."

"How is your new baby sister doing, Gus?" Ms. Diz asked.

Gus shrugged. "It's just like when my little brother was born. Every time Babette burps, my parents think she's a genius."

"It's hard being a big brother," said Ms. Diz.

"It's hard being a little brother, too," I said. "We have to wear used-up big-brother clothes."

I looked down at my own boring shoes. Plain vanilla nothing-special sneakers.

They didn't even light up.

They were from the Ugliest Most Uncool Shoe Warehouse, I am pretty sure.

And my big brother, Max, had already worn them.

They weren't just preworn.

They were prestinked.

When you have to wear your big brother's yucky used clothes, it's called *hand-me-downs*.

Mom says it's also called *watching your spending*.

I am not sure what that means.

Except that it seems to involve making sure your kid will never be cool.

"Class, if we could all stop staring at Hassan's and Coco's feet for a while, we have spelling work to get started on," said Ms. Diz.

"We read you loud and clear, Ms. Diz," said Hassan's right foot.

Everybody laughed.

I would have given anything to have his blisters right about then.

5

Beg-a-thon

When I got home from school, I ran straight into the house.

"Dad! I saw the most miracle thing today!" I screamed.

Dad was in the family room with Hazel, my little sister, and Goofy, my big dog.

Hazel was using Goofy as a pillow.

Dad was using Goofy as a footrest.

They were watching a cartoon about a giraffe with a sore throat. And eating little crackers shaped like fish.

Dad gave me a hug.

Hazel gave me a fishy cracker.

Goofy ate my fishy before I could.

I told Dad how sprouty his bald spot looked.

Then I asked him if he would buy me some Walkie-Talkies.

"What, exactly, are Walkie-Talkies?" he asked.

His eyebrow went up.

That jumping eyebrow means you'd better have a good answer planned.

"There's Walkie-Talkies, Daddy!" Hazel cried.

She pointed to a commercial on TV.

A bunch of kids were talking to their feet.

They looked so happy!

And so cool!

A pair of smiling cartoon sneakers appeared on the screen.

"Trust us, kids!" the right shoe said. "Cool kids walk in shoes that talk!"

"Walkie-Talkies!" said the left shoe. "Get yours today at a store near you! Over and out!"

A new commercial came on. For diapers that don't leak.

The babies on the screen looked happy and cool too.

"See, Dad?" I said. "Aren't they amazing?"

"Uh-oh," said Dad. "Here comes the beg-a-thon."

"What's a beg-a-thon, Daddy?" Hazel asked.

"It's when a kid whines endlessly, but it does no good," said Dad.

"Can I be in the beg-a-thon?" she asked.

"Dad, these shoes are awesome," I said, ignoring Hazel. "And useful. If they make them in giant foot sizes, then you and Mom can get some, and if you are upstairs and she is in the kitchen and she needs you to help her take out the trash, then she can just do this."

I grabbed my left foot and leaned down.

"Harold," I said in my best Mom voice. "Come down here this instant!"

Then I fell over.

Because it is actually not that easy to talk to your foot while you're hopping on the other foot.

Dad just kept staring.

"*Please*, Dad? Please, please, please? I'll clean the garage!"

"The world does not need talking shoes," Dad said. He shook his head. "What's next? Singing underwear?"

"I'll put away groceries till I'm nineteen,"
I said.

"Sorry, guy. I am not spending fifty-nine dollars and ninety-five cents so you can chat with your toes. Especially since you wear out shoes faster than any kid on the planet, Mr. Destructo-feet! You've gone through three pairs of sneakers since school started!"

"I never get cool shoes," I whined.

"You're already cool, Roscoe," said Dad with a grin. "You don't need shoes to prove it!"

"Besides, you have tap shoes," Hazel pointed out.

"That's different," I said. "Those are just for dancing. And everybody in class doesn't want to have a pair!"

Dad shook his head. "Sorry, Roscoe."

I sighed. I flopped on the floor with a groan.

"I just want to be able to talk to my feet!" I cried.

"Over and out," said Dad. His eyebrow went *way* up.

And when Dad's eyebrow says "over," it means *over.*

6

Great-Aunt Imogene to the Rescue

The next morning at school, Coco had on her pink Walkie-Talkies.

Hassan had on his blue lightning Walkie-Talkies.

All the rest of us had on our usual, boring feet.

Maya said, "My mom called six different shoe stores, but no luck. Everybody was sold out. They all said check back next week."

"Everybody wants a pair, I guess," said Coco.

She tied her right shoe while a bunch of us watched.

I have never been jealous of shoe tying before.

"I wore two pairs of socks so my blisters wouldn't hurt so much," Coco said. "But it's worth it."

"I wore about twenty Band-Aids," Hassan agreed.

"Talk to the shoe, Hassan," Coco directed.

"Band-Aids," Hassan repeated into his left toe.

"I asked my mom again if I could get some," Gus said. He sighed. "But she just said 'No means *no*, honey.' And then Babette spit up on her jeans."

"My dad said something about singing underwear," I said.

"What does that mean?" Gus asked.

I watched Coco tie her other shoe.

I sighed, just like Gus. "It means *no* in Dadspeak," I said.

• • •

That afternoon after school, Max and I were in the front yard playing where-did-Goofy-bury-the-Frisbee-this-time.

A big truck parked in front of the house. A man in a brown hat jumped out.

He was carrying a shoebox-sized package and a clipboard.

"Is that for me?" I asked, because you never know.

"That depends," he said. "Are you Master Roscoe Reginald Riley?"

"That's me!" I cried.

"Sign at the X, sir," he said.

I wrote my name very carefully and took the package.

"Who's that from?" Max asked.

He looked at the return address. "Too bad," he said.

I tried to read the handwriting. But it was full of loops and squiggles.

"Why too bad?" I asked.

"It's from Great-aunt Imogene," he said. "Tough luck, kid."

Great-aunt Imogene has about two hundred great-nieces and great-nephews.

Sometimes she gets us mixed up.

She gets birthdays and holidays mixed up too.

Last year she sent me an electric razor for Saint Patrick's Day.

Which was very nice of her.

Except that I am not doing a whole lot of shaving just yet.

The year before that, she sent me a frilly pink ballet tutu.

I gave it to Hazel.

I tore open the box. Inside was a present wrapped in yellow paper.

I opened the card attached to it.

"*Happy Fourteenth Birthday to Roscoe!*" I read out loud. "*With love and kisses from your Great-aunt Imogene.*"

Which was also very nice of her.

Except that my birthday was five and a half months away.

And I will not exactly be fourteen for another eight years.

"Oh, well," Max said with a big-brother grin. "Mom always says it's the thought that counts."

"Remember that time she sent Hazel boxing gloves?" I asked. "And Hazel was only two weeks old?"

I crossed my fingers. Maybe there were boxing gloves in the box.

That would be a big improvement over a tutu.

I tore off a little paper.

I saw a big *W* on the box.

I tore off a little more.

I saw a big *T*.

No way. It couldn't be.

I was afraid to hope.

I closed my eyes and tore off the rest of the paper.

"Whoa," Max said. "Double whoa. Triple whoa."

I opened my eyes.

I would have *whoa*ed along with Max.

But I was too busy screaming for joy.

It was a miracle.

There was no other way to explain it.

Great-aunt Imogene had sent me a pair of bright red, shiny, brand-new, right-size shoes.

I had my very own Walkie-Talkies!

7

Cool at Last

When I climbed onto the bus the next morning, Gus took one look at my feet and his eyes grew giant.

"You got some!" he cried.

We did one of our special secret handshakes.

It's called high five, low five, foot five, no five.

"How did you get those?" Gus asked. "What did you say to your parents?"

"It wasn't my parents. It was my Great-aunt Imogene."

"The one who sent you a teething ring on the Fourth of July?"

"I don't know what happened. It's a total miracle," I said.

"Last night my mom said I have to wait until my sneakers wear out before I can get a new pair," Gus said. "Then Babette threw up on her sweater."

"Why do babies throw up so much?" I asked.

"Dad says they're badly designed," Gus said.

He looked at my shoes with a sad but hopeful face.

The way Goofy looks at a hamburger.

"Don't worry," I said. "Your shoes will wear out in no time."

Gus kicked at the seat in front of us. "I doubt it," he said. "You know what these sneakers are called?"

I shook my head.

He held up a foot so I could read the words on the side of his shoe.

"Ruff and Tuffs," I read.

"You've seen their ad, right?" Gus asked.

I nodded. Poor Gus.

We both said the ad words together: "*Ruff and Tuffs. The shoes that refuse to die!*"

I don't know why, but I stuck my feet under the seat in front of me.

It just felt like the right thing to do.

• • •

As we walked to class, I kept hoping I'd see somebody with a pair of Walkie-Talkies on so I could try out mine.

No luck. Those shoes were as rare as diamonds.

Lots of kids pointed at my feet as I passed by.

Even *big* kids.

The moment I walked into class, Coco saw my shoes and gasped.

"Roscoe Riley!" she screamed. "Where did you get a pair of Walkie-Talkies?"

"My Great-aunt Imogene," I said.

"But where did *she* get them?" Coco demanded.

"I don't know. She lives in New York City. Maybe they have a shoe store there."

Coco seemed a little upset.

I think maybe it was because she didn't want to share any of her coolness.

After all, she'd already had to share it with Hassan.

When Hassan walked in, he saw my shoes and grinned. "Hey, Roscoe, let's try 'em out!"

I tapped the button on my left toe. A fuzzy noise filled the air.

It sounded like our car radio when Dad can't find a station to listen to.

Hassan tapped his toe button too.

Everybody gathered around to see the shoe show.

I felt like a movie star.

Or at least a guy with movie-star shoes.

"It's easier if you sit down," Hassan said.

I sat on a chair. "Testing, one, two, three, four, testing," I said.

And there was my voice, coming out of Hassan's foot!

"Do you hear me?" Hassan asked his toe.

Sure enough, his voice came out of my right shoe!

Of course, I could hear him anyway. On account of he was standing right next to me.

But still. It was about as amazing as shoes can get.

I let everyone have a turn talking to my toe.

It was the first time most of my classmates had gotten a chance to try Walkie-Talkies.

Coco hadn't let anyone try out her shoes.

But I kind of liked all the attention.

Kind of a lot, actually.

Ms. Diz rang her gong. That's the big bellish thing on her desk.

She uses it to say *Time to get to work, kids.* So her voice doesn't get worn out.

Usually the gong works. But today nobody paid any attention.

There were too many kids waiting to talk to my toes.

Ms. Diz said, "I can see we're not going to get anywhere until you get this out of your systems. All right, everybody, line up to chat with Roscoe and Hassan's feet."

I let Gus go first. "Hello," he said. "I wish I had a pair of these so we could talk to each other in class, Roscoe!"

I started to tell Gus he could borrow my shoes anytime.

But the other kids had already pushed him aside so they could have a turn.

He probably wouldn't have heard me, anyway.

There was a whole lot of foot talking going on.

8

Crazy and Annoying

All day long, Coco and Hassan and I were the stars of the class.

Everybody wanted to sit with us.

Everybody wanted to play with us at recess.

Everybody wanted to push the buttons on our magical sneakers.

Near the end of school, Dewan tried to

Walkie-Talkie my foot to say hi to Hassan during math review.

Ms. Diz made a grouchy face.

"Roscoe?" she said. "I need you to turn off your feet, please. Hassan, you too. Those shoes are a bit disruptive."

I didn't mind so much. My toes were a little tired of all the attention.

But by the next morning, they were ready for action again.

It was the same as yesterday. Coco and Hassan and I were like movie stars.

Or baseball heroes.

Or presidents.

Well, maybe we weren't *quite* that cool.

But we weren't ordinary kids anymore.

Especially since nobody else could buy Walkie-Talkies anywhere.

Our shoes sort of united us.

First thing in the morning, we said hi to each other on our shoes.

At lunch, we compared desserts on our shoes.

During music, we sang "Make New Friends, but Keep the Old" on our shoes.

And at recess, we played hide-and-seek, Walkie-Talkie style.

I spent most of recess hiding under the slide.

Hassan and Coco wandered around the playground trying to find me.

"Warmer," I said into my shoe.

"Colder," I said.

Hassan turned one way. Coco went the other.

"You're so cold you are growing nose icicles," I said.

"Hey, Roscoe," said a familiar voice.

I looked up from my hiding place to see Gus.

"Shh," I whispered. "I'm hiding."

"Sorry," Gus said.

"Am I cold or hot?" Hassan asked.

I peeked out.

"You're both at the North Pole, you're so cold," I answered.

Gus sighed. "I'm gonna go swing, I guess. Are you still coming over to my house after school?"

"Of course," I said. "Why wouldn't I?"

"Just thought I'd check," Gus said.

"Roscoe?" my shoe asked. "Am I getting warmer?"

I looked up. There was Hassan. Coco was right behind him.

"Found you! You're it," Hassan said.

"I'm going to go hang out with Gus," I

told Hassan, but just then the bell rang.

"Recess is over, Roscoe!" Hassan said into his sneaker.

I watched Gus trudge away slowly, kicking dirt with his Shoes that Refuse to Die.

"Okay," I said softly. "Over and out."

9

Baby Drool, Foot Sweat, and Other Problems

Mom drove me to Gus's house that afternoon after school.

Gus was sitting on the front porch.

His mom was helping his little brother, Albert, ride a blue plastic trike.

His dad had Babette in a pouch thingie that hung from his chest.

He looked like a kangaroo with a beard.

My mom ran over to make ooh-how-cute noises about the baby.

I ran over to Gus to make ooh-how-gross noises about the baby.

When Mom finally drove off, I am pretty sure she was still oohing in the car.

"So, Roscoe," said Gus's dad, "these are the famous Walkie-Talkies I've heard so much about."

I held up a foot so he could see one.

As he leaned over, Babette drooled on my sock.

I tried not to look shocked.

But I was for sure going to have to throw that sock away when I got home.

"You push this button here," I said. "And if someone else has Walkie-Talkies, you can talk to them."

"Wow," said Gus's dad. "How cool is

that? Do they come in adult sizes?"

"Gary," said Gus's mom, "you're not really helping."

"Oops," said Gus's dad. He winked at Gus. "They are awesome, Gus. When your sneakers wear out, we'll talk about it."

"These are Ruff and Tuffs, Dad. They never wear out," said Gus.

Gus's dad was about to answer, but Babette started crying.

"Gotta change the kid," said Gus's dad.

Just then, Albert tipped over on his trike and skinned his elbow.

He cried even louder than Babette.

"Boys, you two will have to come inside while we take care of the little ones," Gus's mom said.

We followed the two screaming kids and Gus's parents inside.

The house smelled like baby.

"Gus!" his dad said. "Could you bring me some baby wipes? They're in the diaper bag in Babette's room."

"And grab that box of Band-Aids in the bathroom, Gus," added his mom.

"Sometimes I hate being a big brother," Gus muttered.

"I know it's hard, sweetheart," said his mom.

Gus headed up the stairs. A few minutes later, he came back with a box of baby wipes and some Band-Aids.

"Let's go play in my room," he said. "There's too many little kids down here. It's like an alien invasion."

Gus's room was even messier than mine.

I sat down on a pile of dirty clothes and felt right at home.

"I remember when Hazel was a baby," I said. "My parents paid all the attention to her. It was like Max and me didn't even exist."

Gus nodded. "Lately, I feel like I'm invisible."

"You're not invisible to me!" I said.

I tossed a dirty sock at Gus and scored a direct hit.

"There's proof!" I said. "I can see you just fine!"

Gus just lay there.

He didn't even fire the sock back at me.

I had to cheer him up somehow.

"Gus," I said. "I've got a great idea. I want you to wear my Walkie-Talkies for a while. For a whole day, even." I thought for a moment. "No! For a whole entire week!"

Gus sat up on his elbows. "You'd do that for me?"

I kicked off my shoes. "Here. Try them on."

Gus tried to put on my right Walkie-Talkie.

He made a face and shook his head.

"Foot sweat?" I asked.

"No, it's just that my feet are too big to fit."

"Squeeze harder," I said.

Gus tried again. "I feel like Cinderella with the glass slipper."

"Actually, the slipper fit Cinderella. You would be an ugly stepsister," I said.

Finally, Gus managed to squeeze his feet into both shoes.

He stood up. He was a little wobbly, on account of his squished condition.

"Ow," he said. "They're amazing. Ow. But I don't think I could wear them for a whole week. My feet would probably fall off. Thanks, though."

"You'll get some Walkie-Talkies soon, Gus," I said. "Your sneakers have to fall apart eventually, right?"

"I suppose."

"How can shoes refuse to die?" I asked. "Dad says all my sneakers wear out in a week."

I picked up one of the Ruff and Tuffs. "I know what their ads say," I said. "But these sure look like regular old sneakers. I'll bet you I could wear them out in no time!"

"I wish you could," Gus said. "Then I'd finally get my own Walkie-Talkies!"

And that's when it hit me.

I, Mr. Destructo-feet, was the answer to Gus's Walkie-Talkie prayers.

"Gus," I said. "Let me borrow your sneakers for a day. I guarantee you'll need a new pair of shoes in no time, if my feet have anything to say about it!"

10

Destructo-Feet

"Roscoe," my dad said when I got home, "where are your Walkie-Talkies? And whose gigantic shoes are those?"

"They're Gus's," I explained. "He really, really wants a pair of Walkie-Talkies. We're switching for a day."

"How can Gus's feet possibly fit in your shoes?" my mom asked.

"Toe smushing," I explained.

Mom and Dad gave each other a kids-are-crazy look.

All that evening and Saturday morning, I wore Gus's shoes.

I wore them to the playground.

I wore them climbing up to my tree house in the backyard.

I wore them while I played basketball with Max.

And you know what?

Those Ruff and Tuffs got dirty and dusty and dinged up.

But they definitely were not interested in dying anytime soon.

Clearly, I had to get serious.

I ran my fastest.

I jumped my highest.

I kicked the hardest rocks I could find.

But those shoes were still almost as good as new.

By Saturday afternoon, it looked like I was going to have to tell Gus that I'd failed.

"Here," I said when he came over to play. "Take your Ruff and Tuffs back. Turns out they can't be killed. I tried everything."

Gus examined one of his sneakers.

"Amazing," he muttered. "That ad is actually true!"

"I've never seen sneakers like this," I said. "I can't understand it. I did all the things I usually do with my shoes."

Suddenly another one of my great ideas popped into my brain. "Hey," I said with a grin, "maybe we need to try some *un*usual things."

Gus grinned back. "Like what?" he asked.

"Follow me," I said.

I led Gus to the garage and opened my Junior Handyman toolbox.

"Hammer, anyone?" I asked.

Gus chose a blue plastic hammer.

I chose a nice yellow pair of pliers.

"Race you," I said.

Gus hammered his right Ruff and Tuff as hard as he could.

I squeezed and poked his left Ruff and Tuff as hard as I could.

"Boys?" my mom called from the driveway. "What are you up to in there?"

"We're just making something, Mom," I yelled back.

"Unmaking something is more like it," Gus whispered.

"Well, don't make a mess," Mom called.

After five more minutes of hammering and pliering, we checked our work.

Gus shook his head. "These are like Godzilla shoes. They're indestructible."

"Nothing's indestructible, Gus," I said. "Take it from Mr. Destructo-feet."

"What else can we do to them?" Gus asked.

"Scissors?" I suggested.

"Too obvious," Gus said.

"Garbage disposal?"

"Too dangerous," Gus said.

"Toilet flushing?" I said.

Gus made a face. "Too risky."

I threw one of the Ruff and Tuffs at the garage wall.

It bounced right back to me.

Good as new.

"Face it, Roscoe," Gus said. "The shoes beat us, fair and square."

11

Baby Braking

Before Gus went home, I asked him to let me keep the Ruff and Tuffs for one more day.

I just wasn't quite ready to give up yet.

It's hard to accept defeat.

Especially when you get beaten by a sneaker.

I sat near the garage, holding Gus's

sneakers in my hands. Wondering where I'd gone wrong.

Hazel was riding her pink bike up and down the driveway.

She was singing "How Much Is that Froggie in the Window?"

I watched her come and go.

It's a long driveway, with a little bit of a hill.

Hazel had to brake pretty hard when she got to the bottom.

Her tires left a black mark on the cement.

Aha, I thought.

I ran to get my bike out of the garage.

"I have only just begun to fight," I said.

I laced up Gus's Ruff and Tuffs and climbed onto my bike.

I sped down the driveway at top speed.

"Slow down, Roscoe!" Hazel called.

I slowed down, all right.

But I didn't use my pedals to brake.

I used my Destructo-feet!

I dragged those Ruff and Tuffs along the cement and stopped just in the nick of time.

"Roscoe," Hazel said. "That's how babies stop their bikes."

But I didn't care.

When I got back to the top of the hill, I checked my handiwork.

"Yes!!!" I screamed.

The toes were scuffed!

Tiny little holes were starting!

Victory at last!

I went down the hill again, sneaker-braking for the last half.

"Brothers are so weird," Hazel muttered.

After ten more rides, the Ruff and Tuffs were looking quite scraggly.

Suddenly I had a gulp moment.

I thought about Gus's mom and dad seeing the destructo-ed Ruff and Tuffs.

What if they weren't so happy about Gus's shoes dying?

Oh, well, I thought. I was just trying to make Gus feel better.

And like Mom always says, it's the thought that counts.

Besides, it was too late to turn back now.

I went down that driveway thirty-two more times.

After ride number thirty-two, I checked Gus's sneakers again.

The Shoes that Refuse to Die were going to need a funeral.

12
Everybody's Cool

Monday morning I had a dentist appointment for a tooth cleaning.

I wore a new pair of jeans that were a little too long for me so that Gus's messed-up shoes wouldn't catch my mom's attention.

I had the feeling she would not be happy about the dead Ruff and Tuffs.

I chose bubble-gum flavor for my tooth rinse.

The dentist said try to brush those back teeth more.

She gave me a travel toothbrush and some floss for a prize.

Which any kid will tell you is a lame reward.

Mom dropped me off at school after the dentist.

I ran straight to class extra fast.

At least, as fast as I could go, wearing floppy shoes that were ripped to shreds.

As I reached for the door to class, I heard Ms. Diz doing something unusual.

She was yelling.

Loudly.

"These shoes are going to drive me crazy!" she said.

Wow, I thought. *Coco and Hassan and Gus must really be having fun with their Walkie-Talkies!*

I opened the door.

It wasn't Coco. Or Hassan. Or Gus.

It was *everyone*!

Everyone was wearing a pair of Walkie-Talkies!

Even Emma.

I saw pink Walkie-Talkies and silver Walkie-Talkies and even polka-dot Walkie-Talkies.

Feet were talking to feet all over the place.

"Roscoe, we missed you!" Ms. Diz said when I entered. She looked down at my feet. "Where are your Walkie-Talkies? Everyone else seems to have a pair!"

She rubbed her forehead. She closed her eyes.

The noise was deafening.

Gus ran over to do our secret handshake.

He had on Walkie-Talkies too, but they weren't mine. They were yellow with orange stripes!

"When my mom saw me wearing your Walkie-Talkies, she said she realized how much I wanted a pair of my own. And then she found out they got a big shipment of them at Shoe-mart," he said. "Isn't this amazing? It's like the whole world has a pair! Now we're all cool!"

"Amazing," I said.

"I put yours in my cubby. Go get them, so we can talk to each other!" Gus said. "Hey, that reminds me. Did you bring my Ruff and Tuffs? Because Mom said she'd get me these if I save my old sneakers for Albert."

I pulled up my jeans a little. "These *are* your Ruff and Tuffs," I said softly.

Gus stared. And stared.

I think he may have said something. But I couldn't hear him above all the Walkie-Talkie noise.

"What . . . what happened?" Gus finally asked.

"They died," I said.

Gus opened his mouth, but instead of his voice, I heard Principal Goosegarden.

He was talking out of the loudspeaker on the wall.

We all got very quiet.

"Attention, students!" he said. "Effective immediately, the shoes known as Walkie-Talkies are banned from our school. We regret this, but we have decided that they are simply causing too much noise during class. If you are currently wearing these sneakers, please remove them. They may be worn today only for gym, recess, and lunch, and when you leave school. Tomorrow, any person wearing these . . . these extremely noisy shoes will be sent home to change. That is all."

We sat there in silence.

Shocked.

Ms. Diz did a hoot of happiness. She threw her fist in the air.

"Yes!" she said. "Go, Goosegarden!"

I think maybe then she noticed all our unhappy faces.

Because she settled down and said, "I'm sorry about this, children, but it's for the best. Please put your shoes in your cubbies, and we'll get right to work."

I pulled off Gus's Ruff and Tuffs.

"But Roscoe's feet stink!" Coco protested.

I checked. "They just smell feety," I reported.

"I finally got to be cool," Gus said. "And it only lasted for one morning."

"Don't worry, Gus," I said. "Being cool's not all it's cracked up to be. Besides, we can wear our Walkie-Talkies when we hang out together after school."

"Not after our moms see those Ruff and Tuffs," Gus said. "We're going to be in time-out till we're ninety-four."

13

Good-Bye from Time-Out

Fortunately, I don't have to be in time-out till I'm ninety-four.

And neither does Gus.

But I do have to be here for a little while.

And I have to clean out the garage and carry in the groceries forever.

Also, Gus and I have to pay for his

Ruff and Tuffs.

He says I'm still the best buddy in the world.

Destructo-feet and all.

You know, I kind of wish I'd never even heard of Walkie-Talkies.

The coolness has definitely worn off those sneakers, if you know what I mean.

That's okay. Having the newest, coolest shoes isn't as big a deal as I thought it would be.

Although, speaking of new and cool, I *did* see an interesting ad on TV this morning.

It was for a backpack that displays light-up messages.

You can program it to say HI!

Or WHAT'S NEW?

Or ROSCOE RILEY RULES!

It's available at fine stores everywhere! And it's only thirty-nine dollars and ninety-five cents!

I'm going to ask my parents if I can get one.

Really, how could they say no?

10 THINGS I WONDER ABOUT BEFORE I FALL ASLEEP AT NIGHT

by Me, Roscoe Riley

1. Cauliflower: good for you.
Candy: not so good.
How exactly is that fair?

2. Do fish keep swimming when they sleep?

3. Why does some cheese smell like feet?

4. If yo-yos and boomerangs come back, why can't Frisbees and footballs?

5. Why do dads snore louder than moms?

6. How come recess goes too fast, but spelling tests go on forever?

7. Why was baby drool invented?

8. Why does my big brother always get to be older than me? Couldn't we take turns?

9. I and eye. See and sea. How come spelling words get to be so tricky?

10. When Mom and Dad say, "No, we will not buy you that new backpack," do they maybe just this once mean "maybe"?

Turn the page for a
super-special sneak peek
at my next adventure!

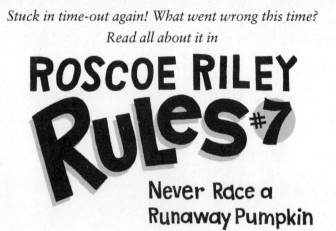

ROSCOE RILEY Rules #7

Never Race a Runaway Pumpkin

Sometimes I wish I hadn't gone to the school library last week.

Then I never would have seen the giant pumpkin that got me into so much trouble.

Don't get me wrong. I love our school library.

It's the most fun place in my school.

Except maybe for the playground.

Our library has maps. And DVDs. And CDs. And computers.

But most of all, it has tons of books.

My class goes there twice a week for story time.

Our story-time area is shaped like a little pirate ship. On the deck are lots of squishy pillows.

Mr. Page is the library helper who reads to us.

He has the best name for a library guy, I think.

Although Mr. Shhh would be good too.

When Mr. Page reads, he wears a black eye patch like a real pirate.

Also, he says, "ARGHH, me hearties!"

Which is Pirate for *Hello, kids!*

This time Mr. Page was wearing an orange eye patch, though.

On account of the book he was going to read us was about pumpkins.

"Okay, folks," said Mr. Page. "Today's

book is called *Pumpkin Power*. It's full of fun facts about pumpkins."

He held up the book. The cover had a picture of a giant pumpkin on it.

"Before we start reading," said Mr. Page, "I want to tell you about an even bigger pumpkin!"

He unrolled a poster.

There was a photo of a boy and a girl on it.

They were each holding a book. And smiling.

And next to them was the most gigantic pumpkin I had ever seen. It looked huge!

It was as tall as my dad.

Almost.

And as big as our car.

Almost.

"That's got to be the world's biggest

pumpkin," I cried.

"Actually, giant pumpkins can reach over one thousand six hundred pounds," said Mr. Page. "This one is gigantic, all right. But it's not *that* big."

"Any kind of gigantic is good, if you ask me," I said.

"This poster is from Hilltop Bookstore," Mr. Page said. "They're having a contest. If you guess the weight of the giant pumpkin in their window, you win books for the school library. Enough to fill that giant pumpkin!"

"That's a lot of books!" said Emma.

"You're right, Emma. And we sure could use them," said Mr. Page. "You can make a guess when you visit the bookstore. The winner will be announced at the Fall Festival on Saturday."

"I'll bet that pumpkin weighs two hundred buzillion pounds!" Hassan said.

"Nunh-uh," said Gus. "Seven thousand katrillion pounds, at least."

Emma said, "I'm not sure if buzillion and katrillion are for-real numbers. But googol is a real number, right, Ms. Diz?"

Ms. Diz is our first-grade teacher.

She knows lots of math and spelling.

And also how to wiggle her ears.

"Googol *is* a number, Emma," Ms. Diz said. "A very big number. It has one hundred zeros in it!"

"That pumpkin is for sure a googol pounds then," I said.

"Children," said Ms. Diz, "maybe we should work on estimating how much things weigh. It could be a wonderful learning opportunity."

When Ms. Diz says learning opportunity, she gets very excited.

She is a brand-new teacher, so she likes to try out new ideas on us. Mostly that is a good thing.

But once she let us make marshmallow crispies so we could learn about measuring.

After that Learning Opportunity, she had to send home a letter to all the parents about How to Wash Marshmallow Goo out of Your Child's Hair.

"Kids, I forgot to mention that the contest winner also gets a prize," added Mr. Page. "Candy. Lots of it. Enough to fill the pumpkin."

"A googol pounds of candy!" said Gus.

He had a goofy smile on his face.

I probably did too.

"ARGHH, me hearties!" said Mr. Page

in his pirate voice. "It's time to read!"

He held up the book so we could see the first page.

"'You may think that a pumpkin is a vegetable,'" he read. "'But it's really a fruit, because it has seeds inside of it.'"

Hmm, I thought. It was a very interesting fact.

But not nearly as interesting as the news about the contest.

Mr. Page kept on reading about pumpkins. He talked about giant pumpkins, tiny pumpkins, pumpkin seeds, and pumpkin pie.

My ears tried to pay attention.

But my brain kept thinking how nice it would be to win books for the library.

And candy for me.

Katherine Applegate is not, has never been, and most likely never will be the coolest kid in school. She will never be accused of setting fashion trends either, and that's just fine with her. Her husband, two kids, dogs, guinea pigs, and cat like her just the way she is. She is the author of many books for children and lives in California.